721

The Victorians

This book has been designed to bring
Victorian history to life. The story and pictures
provide children with a useful insight into the
period. However, this is not intended
to be a history text book.

The story and pictures in this book are
all original and have been specially
commissioned for Tesco.

Published for
Tesco Stores Limited
by Brilliant Books Ltd
84-86 Regent Street
London W1R 6DD

First published 1998

Printed by Cambus Litho Ltd, Scotland
Reproduction by Graphic Ideas Studios, England

fun to learn

collection

The Victorians

Edited by Michael Rosen

Illustrated by Andy Hammond

Alfie was fed up. His family were arguing about what to watch on TV, and he wasn't interested in any of the programmes. He wandered down to the old garden shed at the bottom of his garden. Maybe, if he rummaged about in the junk down there, something mysterious might happen…

Underneath an ancient looking typewriter, that he'd been examining, Alfie found an old letter with a one penny black stamp on it. Inside the envelope was a letter and a very old third-class train ticket. As he unfolded the stiff yellowish paper, he felt that familiar dizzy feeling and knew immediately he was going to have another one of his trips back in time!

The next thing Alfie knew, he was in total darkness.
He stepped forward and banged his head on something.
Dust showered down on him. "I must be in a mine!"
he thought. There was no air and Alfie started to panic.
But at that moment, he saw a dim light in the distance.
"Help! Help!" yelled Alfie.
"Wait a moment," a voice answered cheerfully.
    The light got nearer and a boy with a
        filthy face appeared.

"Hello, I'm Tim. Are you alright?"

"Yes, I think so," said Alfie. "I'm Alfie and..."
He was suddenly interrupted by a heavy rumbling
sound. The ground shook under them.

"Quick, follow me!" said Tim, grabbing Alfie by the
arm. They raced along a dark dusty tunnel. As they ran,
Alfie could feel the roar and rumble following them.

"Daylight! Thank goodness!" thought Alfie,
as they burst out into the open air.
"...Another roof-fall," said Tim, looking back.
   Standing nearby was a fat, smartly dressed
man shouting at some anxious looking men.
"This mine is perfectly safe! Now get back
to work or I'll sack the lot of you!"
"He's Mr Dweeb – the mine owner!" whispered Tim.
   "Twelve people died last year and a friend of mine
      was killed last month," he said sadly.
      "He was only ten. Mr Dweeb didn't even
      give his mother the wages he was owed.
      He pays me a shilling a week,
      and I work a 12 hour shift!"
      Alfie was shocked. He knew that
      a shilling was only 5p!

Alfie walked back with Tim to his home.
Everywhere he looked, people seemed so thin
and sad. Their clothes were like rags and their
shoes had holes in them. But every now and again,
a grand Victorian carriage clattered past,
full of people dressed in fine clothes.
When they arrived at Tim's house,
Alfie was horrified, it was as run down as all
the rest. The front door was made out of old
bits of wood nailed together and several
of the windows were broken.

Inside, a worried looking
woman was nursing a young
boy, who was coughing badly.

"My brother's very ill and we don't have
enough money for his medicine," Tim said.

"Tim, go and clean yourself up," said his
mother. "You'll find some soup in the bottom
of the pot and the crust from yesterday's loaf."

Tim and Alfie went outside. "Look at
this, Alfie," Tim said. "It's a model of the
first steam train. It was a week's wages. But
my mum says I've got to sell it to buy food."

Alfie admired it, but felt sorry for Tim.

Alfie had just finished cleaning himself
up, when he remembered the old letter.
Tim saw him start to read it.
"Can you read?" he asked.
"Of course I can!" said Alfie.
"Oh," said Tim. "I can't. I only went
to school for a few years and then I had to
    go and work down the mines."
        Tim went to get some of the soot off him,
            leaving Alfie to look at the letter.

20 South Street
Newcastle

24 June 1852

Dear Mr Dweeb,

My engineers have reported back to me after inspecting your mine. I regret to say, that on no account should you proceed to open up the new west shaft.

It would be extremely dangerous – not only would it be unsafe, but it would probably cause the collapse of the whole mine.

I am sorry not to give you better news, but to pursue your plans would lead to many of your miners losing their lives.

Yours faithfully
Robert Stephenson

Alfie shouted to Tim, asking if the new shaft had been opened up. "No, but the men are blasting it open with explosives tonight," said Tim. Alfie begged Tim not to go down the mine that night, but Tim refused; "I've got to go – I'll lose my job if I don't."

Alfie decided that he would have to go and
see Mr Dweeb – maybe he had never even
got the letter. He asked Tim where he lived.
"You can't go there!" said Tim.
"The servants will turn you away!"
Eventually, Tim agreed to take Alfie to
Mr Dweeb's house. He lived in a smart square
in a great big house. His gleaming carriage was
outside. Just as Alfie summoned up the courage
to knock on the door, it was opened by a butler.

Mr Dweeb stepped out, holding his stick.
"Get out of my way!" he snapped at Alfie.
"But, I have a letter for you, sir," said Alfie.
Mr Dweeb snatched it out of his hand, read it,
then crumpled it up and put it into his pocket.
"This is rubbish. My mine is perfectly safe.
Now clear off and don't bother me again!"
Alfie was shocked. Mr Dweeb had paid no
attention to the letter at all!
Dozens of miners could be
killed – including poor Tim!
"What can I do?" he thought.

Perhaps Mr Stephenson could do something to stop Mr Dweeb? Alfie remembered his address from the letter and Tim knew where the street was. They set off to see the engineer, but the news was bad. Mr Stephenson had gone to Whitby for the weekend. They had no money and there was no way they could get to Whitby.

"Hang on a minute!" thought Alfie, "I've still got the train ticket! I'll go to Whitby and find him!" Alfie told Tim to warn the miners about the shaft and rushed off to the station.

Alfie waited on the platform as a great steam
train stopped beside him with an enormous hiss.
Even though he only had a third-class ticket his
carriage was very clean. With a lot of noise and
puffing, the steam train started to move. First, they
chugged past some factories pouring smoke into
the air, then they puffed passed rows of dirty looking
terraced houses. But soon they were steaming
through some of the most beautiful
countryside Alfie had seen.

At Whitby, Alfie leapt off the train and made
his way to the seafront. All the people on the
beach were wearing very funny bathing-suits
and were rushing in and out of little huts on
wheels, parked in the sand. Alfie walked
along the beach asking if anyone knew
a Mr Stephenson, but no one did.

Just as Alfie was about to give up, a man said,
"I'm Robert Stephenson. How can I help?"
Mr Stephenson listened to Alfie's story and was
horrified. "I'm afraid that Mr Dweeb's like a lot
of businessmen these days – he only cares about
making more money. If men die, it doesn't
concern him very much. I think we should
pay him a visit. I'm rather bored here
anyway," he said smiling.

Mr Stephenson bought the return tickets.
He was obviously quite important since
everyone was very polite to him.
Alfie decided to ask if he was famous.
"It's my father you probably know. I helped
him build the first steam train: 'Locomotion'.
I was still quite young, but since then I've
designed railways and bridges all over the
country," said Mr Stephenson smiling.
When they arrived at Newcastle, they stopped
at the police station and Mr Stephenson
asked two policemen to come with
them to see Mr Dweeb.

They had to get to the mine before the men on the
night shift set off the explosions to open up the new
shaft – otherwise lots of miners would die! It was
already getting dark. As they arrived at the pithead,
they heard a loud boom coming from under the
ground. They were too late! Mr Stephenson
leapt out of the coach, raced over to the
entrance to the mine and shouted.
"Get out! Everyone out!"

Just then, Mr Dweeb arrived. "What the
Dickens are you doing?" he shouted.
"I'm getting the men out of your mine,"
answered Mr Stephenson firmly, "because as
you well know, Mr Dweeb, it's not safe."

"You'll do no such thing!" screamed Mr Dweeb.
"I'm paying those lay-abouts to get MY coal out
of MY mine and YOU'RE not going to stop me!"
Mr Dweeb suddenly lashed out at Mr Stephenson!
There was a scuffle, but the policemen grabbed him and led
him away. At that moment, there was another loud rumble...

Alfie and Mr Stephenson looked at each other
anxiously. At last, a group of miners staggered out
of the pit, coughing and spluttering. Alfie was just
wondering if Tim was alright when someone tugged
his sleeve – it was Tim! "We were lucky to get out
of there," he said. "The whole west shaft caved in!"
Alfie was telling Tim how he had found
Mr Stephenson, when he saw a big gold watch
lying on the ground. "Mr Dweeb must have
dropped it during the scuffle," said Alfie.
"I reckon it's a case of finders keepers," said
Mr Stephenson, beaming. "I've got to go
down to the police station now. Goodbye."

"Tim, you should have this watch and sell it to buy some medicine for your little brother," said Alfie. Tim refused – "I can't, it must be worth a fortune!" But Alfie insisted and eventually Tim took it, saying, "I'll try to repay you one day. Thank you." He ran off waving goodbye.

Alfie was exhausted and sat down. The next thing he knew, he was back in the garden shed. Something was digging into his leg. He reached into his pocket and found Tim's train!